SUE PURKISS

Spooks Away

Illustrated by Lynne Chapman

A & C Black · London

First published 2005 by
A & C Black Publishers Ltd
37 Soho Square, London, W1D 3QZ

www.acblack.com

ISBN-10: 0-7136-7419-9
ISBN-13: 978-0-7136-7419-4

A CIP catalogue for this book is available from the British Library.

A & C Black uses paper produced with elemental chlorine-free
pulp, harvested from managed sustained forests.

Printed and bound in Great Britain by Bookmarque Ltd, Croydon

Chapter One

It was *sooo* hard getting up for the first day of term after the long summer holiday. Spooker Batt, ghost-in-training, turned over and buried his head under his pillow, hoping the noise and the nagging would go away…

'Spooker, it's time you were up!' called his father.

The door was flung open and an exceptionally mean person opened the curtains, letting the evening light flood in, and saying in a *very* loud voice:

'Come along, dear, you don't want to be late, do you?' It was his mother.

Despite all this, Spooker was just managing to have a last little snooze when a terrible screaming noise invaded his ears. He leapt out of bed to find that his little sister Phanta had put her alarm clock right beside his head, and was smiling sweetly at him from the doorway.

It didn't get any better. Nothing was where he'd put it at the end of last term. School bag, pencil case, lunch box – everything had vanished. But finally, after a heroic effort, Spooker was ready. He hurtled out of the front door, and breathed a sigh of relief when he saw that his best friends, Holly and Goof, were still waiting for him. There was a lot to catch up on.

They were so busy talking that they hardly noticed the walk, and in no time at all the ghosts were entering the gates of the Anne Boleyn Secondary School.

As they went through the playground, Spooker noticed that a group of girls was looking at him. There was nudging and giggling, and a lot of sideways glances.

'What's going on?' he asked, puzzled.

He looked down at himself. Perhaps in the rush he'd put his jumper on inside out, or maybe he had toothpaste on his face.

Holly grinned. 'It's because you're famous,' she said.

'Yes – you're a hero,' said Goof solemnly. 'Can I have your autograph?'

Then Spooker understood. Of *course*.

After the school inspection by Ofghost at the end of the summer term, there had been an article about him in the local paper. The In-spectres had made one or two criticisms of the school. In particular, they'd singled out Sir Rupert Grimsdyke, who'd been the practical haunting teacher for many years.

Practical haunting was the most important subject on the curriculum, because it did exactly what it said; it taught ghosts all the techniques they needed for haunting. But Sir Rupert had had some very old-fashioned ideas about haunting; he liked to frighten people – humans or ghosts, he wasn't fussy. And as it turned out the In-spectres didn't approve of his methods – 'absolutely abysmal' had been the kindest phrase they'd used.

Spooker, on the other hand, had come in for a good deal of praise. The In-spectres had seen the practical haunting he'd done for his exams. Spooker wasn't very good at being frightening, so instead he'd made friends with Ben, the boy he was supposed to haunt, and decided to use his haunting skills to help him.

The In-spectres had been so impressed by Spooker's approach that they'd singled him out at the end of the inspection. He'd been called up on stage in front of the whole school, which was very embarrassing, as was his mention in the paper. Spooker had hoped everyone would have forgotten about it by now, but clearly they hadn't.

Fortunately, just then the Banshee appeared to ring the bell. She backed it up with her speciality wail, and everyone stuck their fingers in their ears as they set off to their new classrooms.

'Wonder who we've got for a tutor this year,' said Holly, as they walked along the corridor. 'It should have been Sir Rupert, shouldn't it?'

'Yeah, but thanks to you, Spooks, we've got rid of him,' said Goof.

After Ofghost's visit, Sir Rupert had left, much to everyone's relief. The rumour was he had headed for Hollywood, hoping to make a career in special effects.

Spooker grinned. 'Well, it wasn't all to do with me. But anyway — it was a pleasure!'

Their new tutor was waiting for them when they arrived at their classroom. They studied her with interest. She was slightly less ancient than some of the staff, but she was still a long way from being young and trendy. She was wearing a neat blouse, tucked into a plain skirt, with a shapeless cardigan over the top. Her hair was whipped up into a sort of copper-coloured beehive and her mouth was set in a thin straight line. But her eyes were the oddest thing. They were almost hidden behind a pair of batwing glasses with thick, tinted lenses.

She turned to look at Spooker as he came in, but all he could see was his own reflection. It was curiously disturbing, not being able to see her eyes. Like looking into two murky pools, which might have anything hidden in their depths – sharks, Loch Ness monsters, rusty tin cans… Something about her made him feel uneasy.

'And your name is?' she enquired.

'Spooker Batt, Miss,' he said.

'Ah! The famous and fabulous Master Batt, hero of the inspection! I was reading about you just now – there's a newspaper cutting on display outside the head's office. So young, but oh so famous. What an honour to meet you.'

She smiled. It wasn't a nice smile.

The class was quiet, waiting to see what their new teacher was going to be like.

She gazed round, and then began to speak:

'My name is Miss Ravilius. I am here to teach practical haunting, in place of Sir Rupert, who I believe left rather suddenly.' She glanced at Spooker, and went on, 'I am to be your tutor this year. However, I'm afraid you will have to manage without me next week. It appears that the In-spectres were so impressed by Master Batt's practical haunting abilities that they have provided funding for a small group – including, of course, himself – to spend a week away from school making a video. The idea, I believe, is that the video will show an example of Master Batt's skills, and that this will be used to … well, to inspire students in other schools. As I am an expert in the subject, your headmaster, Mr White, asked me to accompany the group to Inverscreech Castle in Scotland. And I was only too happy to agree.'

She smiled at Spooker. 'You'll like Inverscreech, I'm sure. It's a place which is full of atmosphere. Very inspiring. You're extremely fortunate. I believe the school has used it in the past for residentials, and I myself have taken groups there on many occasions.

'We'll speak more of this later. But now, it is time for assembly. Everyone to the hall, if you please.'

Spooker didn't feel inspired. In fact, a week in a distant castle with Miss Ravilius for company had about as much appeal as a week in a snake-infested pit. He had a bad feeling about his new teacher already. But perhaps he was jumping to conclusions. Perhaps she was really nice when you got to know her. Perhaps – but he thought he'd rather not have the opportunity to find out.

However, by the time Spooker was home and telling his mother all about it, he was feeling more cheerful.

'The bad bit is that we've got this awful woman with a silly name and nasty glasses going with us,' he said, 'but the good bit is that Mr White said I could choose two people to come with me, so Goof and Holly are coming too.'

Dawn was breaking, and Mrs Batt was closing the curtains to keep the light out.

Switching on a lamp, she said, 'I'm not sure that's how you should be talking about your teachers, dear.'

'*I* think Miss Ravilius is really good,' observed Phanta. 'We had a lesson with her today, and she showed us how to do head removal. She says it takes a lot of skill, and

10

everyone needs to be able to do it. It's not about frightening people, it's about being truthful to the spirit of the period. So if your haunting is to do with Anne Boleyn, or Mary Queen of Scots, you have to be ready to take your head off. Some people weren't very good at it, but *I* got the hang of it straight away, so she gave me a merit. Look, shall I show you? Look, Mummy, look at me!'

'Very nice, dear,' said Mrs Batt. 'But put it back on again now, I don't want blood on the carpet. It's so difficult to get the stain out.'

'You're such a creep,' muttered Spooker, glaring at his sister. 'But honestly, Mum, there's something funny about her. I wish another teacher was coming with us.'

'Well, at least it's not going to cost anything for you to go,' said Mrs Batt. 'How are you getting there?' For places that were fairly close, ghosts generally hopped from their dimension to the human one, but that didn't work for long distances.

'Switching dimensions to Parkway and then getting the people train,' said Spooker. 'Chalky – Mr White – says it'll be good for people watching. Useful experience.'

His mother frowned. 'Well, yes, but you must be careful. There are some funny types about nowadays. I'd rather you went by Spectrerail, but I suppose it's a bit slow.' Ghost trains were usually steam trains, and sometimes they had to do a haunting, so they weren't a very quick way to travel. 'Now, whose turn is it to set the table?'

But funnily enough, when she looked up from her newspaper, the room was quite empty.

Chapter Two

It was late Sunday evening, and Miss Ravilius, Spooker, Goof and Holly were waiting in a shadowy corner of Parkway railway station.

'It's not very busy, is it?' said Goof, sounding disappointed. 'We'll have a job to do much people watching. I mean, it's a bit tricky without any people!'

The light gleamed on Miss Ravilius's glasses as she looked towards him. 'It's night-time, Guthrum. Most people are now tucked up safely in their cosy little beds, in their nice little houses. Bless them.'

Spooker turned to look at Goof. '*Guthrum?*'

Goof looked very uncomfortable. 'My grandfather specialised in Viking haunts. You know – ship burials, ancient battles, big helmets, that kind of thing. He was always spouting sagas after tea. I think they hoped

I'd take after him. But nobody *ever* calls me that.' He glared at Miss Ravilius, who didn't appear to notice.

'It's not that bad a name,' said Holly. 'In fact it's quite distinguished. Oh look, the train's coming! It says so on that sign thing.'

'Where?' said Miss Ravilius. 'What sign?'

'Up there.' Holly pointed to a small screen, which showed details of train departures. 'Look, it says the 11.43 for Edinburgh is about to arrive, and…'

'*Edinburgh*?' said their teacher, looking suspiciously at the sign with its changing display. 'But we're not going to Edinburgh, we're going to Inverscreech. I *knew* we should have gone by Spectrerail!'

'No, it's all right,' said Holly, watching the screen. 'We have to change trains at Edinburgh, that's all.'

The train roared in, and soon the ghosts had found seats. Miss Ravilius clearly didn't want to talk, and the others were quite happy to go along with that. Spooker and Goof played cards, while Holly found a magazine that someone had left behind. It was all about celebrities. Film stars invited her into their

14

beautiful homes, and she read about star-studded parties, who was getting married – or divorced – and admired pictures of famous babies. It was all very interesting.

It was early morning when they reached Edinburgh, and they were getting tired. But they woke up quickly when they emerged from the train. Murky grey daylight filtered into the huge, bustling station.

Spooker, Goof and Holly had all done a fair bit of practical haunting, so they were used to being in a house with just a few people. This was a very different matter. It was most disturbing having people continually push through them or brush them aside without a 'sorry' or an 'excuse me'.

'They're so rude!' gasped Holly.

'I don't think it's that,' said Spooker, bouncing back after being run through by a big man in a black suit, wielding a particularly fearsome umbrella. 'They just can't see us.'

'They'd see us with a vengeance if I had my way,' muttered Miss Ravilius, as a group of chattering girls breezed through her, wrapping their scarves more tightly round their necks at the sudden chill. 'But we mustn't be nasty to the nice people, must we, Spooker – isn't that what you think? Holly, you seem to be good with this new-fangled technology. For goodness' sake, find out where we've got to go and let's get on with it!'

Holly led the way to Platform 2, where it was much quieter. Goof and Spooker went to investigate the chocolate machine, and Miss Ravilius smoothed her hair and took off her glasses to give them a polish.

At that moment, Holly happened to glance at her teacher's eyes, and was so startled by what she saw that she spoke without thinking. 'Goodness!' she said. 'Are you all right, Miss? Your eyes look really sore!'

Sore was an understatement. The whites of her eyes were horribly bloodshot.

'Don't make personal comments about your teachers, girl!' snapped Miss Ravilius, hastily putting her glasses back on. 'It's just an allergy. To trains. And to all these people. And oh, for the love of Mike, here's more of them, and these ones are American – just *listen* to the noise they're making!'

Holly edged away from her and went to find Spooker and Goof. 'She's so *touchy*!' she complained. 'I was only being nice and she had a real go at me!'

'Perhaps she's just nervous,' said Spooker, 'I don't know why she agreed to come. You can see she's hating every minute of it.'

Goof was watching the people who'd just come onto the platform. There were two men. One was whip thin and dressed elegantly in black. A lock of hair fell becomingly across his forehead. The other was tall and shabby with a long wool scarf and metal-rimmed glasses. The third person was a girl, dressed in a black trouser suit and pointed shoes with heels like daggers. Her hair was glossy and smart, her face was perfectly made up, and she had a mobile phone in one hand, which she was waving about furiously as she carried on a lively argument with the shorter man.

The tall man was weighed down with several heavy-looking black bags. Ignoring the other two, he dumped the bags down on the platform, sat on one, fished a newspaper out of his pocket and began to read.

'Now this is what I call people watching!' whispered Holly, and they moved nearer.

'I *told* you we should've hired a car at the airport!' the woman said angrily.

'And *I* told *you* that to hire a car you need an international driving licence – which of course you forgot!'

'*I* forgot? And what about you, you jumped up little food arranger?'

'You know perfectly well my nerves won't stand for driving – especially on the wrong side of the road – and how dare you call me a ... a ... what you did! I'm a stylist to the stars,' said the man proudly. 'And what do you do? Make phone calls – constantly – and mess up arrangements!'

'How *dare* you! I'm indispensable to Maria. The one who makes a mess of things is *you*!'

The man tossed his head. 'Well, when your boss and mine tie the knot – and *why* they want to do it in this *miserable* little apology for a country is just *so* beyond me – one of us will have to go. And it most certainly will *not* be me!'

The other man folded his paper and stood up. He glanced in the direction of the ghosts and frowned, looking slightly puzzled. Then, looking down the track, he said, 'I guess this is the train. Maybe you two might like to quit arguing and help with these bags?'

'Wow!' breathed Holly. 'Did you hear that? One of them said he was a stylist to the stars! I bet they're from Hollywood. I wonder who he knows?'

'Nobody much. They sounded like a pair of posers to me,' said Spooker.

They didn't have a chance to find out any more. Miss Ravilius made them find seats as far away from the Americans as possible.

'Ghastly people,' she muttered. 'Wonder where they're going. Still, so long as they're not within a hundred miles of Inverscreech, I really don't care.

'Ah, Inverscreech – the peace and quiet, the dark dungeons, the squeak of the bats, the screech of the raven, the howls of people in pain…'

'What?' said Spooker, startled.

'Oh, nothing, nothing. I was just remembering some of the hauntings my old pupils did when I brought them here. Now *they* were excellent students…'

The train, smaller and shabbier than the first one, clattered on through the Highlands. It had been a long night and, after a while, the rhythmic click-clack of the wheels sent all the ghosts gently off to sleep.

Chapter Three

The ghosts slept through the first few stops the little train made, but they were woken by the familiar sound of the Americans shouting at each other. It appeared the ghosts weren't the only ones getting off the train at Inverscreech.

'This *cannot* be the place! Tell me I'm dreaming! There's *nothing* here!'

'If *you're* in it, it's more likely to be a nightmare!'

Then a third, weary voice:

'Guys, do you think maybe peace could break out? Because we've got a job to do, and correct me if I'm wrong, but I don't think arguing is going to help...'

Unfortunately the ghosts were too busy collecting their things and tumbling out onto the platform to hear any more.

'I don't believe it! Of all the stations in all the towns in all of Scotland, why did they

have to end up in the same one as us!'
grumbled Miss Ravilius.

'I wonder what they're doing here?' said
Holly. 'It's an odd place for people from
Hollywood to come.'

'I don't know and I don't care. Now shape
up, all of you. You have the coordinates – let's
switch dimensions and get to the castle!'

Then she promptly disappeared.

Goof looked at the space where Miss
Ravilius had been. 'You were right, Spooker,'
he said sadly, 'this is going to be grim, isn't it?'

Spooker agreed. 'She doesn't like us, she
doesn't like people and she doesn't like
travelling. I only hope she knows something
about making videos – otherwise, I don't see
the point of her being here at all.'

'She must do,' said Holly hopefully. 'After
all, she is a teacher, isn't she? Anyway, I can
use a video camera – they're easy. Come on,
let's go see this castle. And cheer up, it's got
to be better than school!'

'Look!' said Miss Ravilius, suddenly
sounding brighter as she gazed into the
distance. 'Isn't it just gorgeous?'

The castle was outlined in dark, brooding splendour against the sky. Some kinds of stone are a creamy or golden colour, and reflect light; Inverscreech was built of deep grey granite, which did the opposite – it absorbed the light. In fact, it seemed to have drained the light from the sun itself. Dark clouds rolled across the sky to make a forbidding backdrop to the tall tower, which loomed up in the centre of the castle.

'It's a bit gloomy, isn't it,' said Goof doubtfully.

'Gloomy? *Gloomy*? Of *course* it's gloomy. It's perfect for a haunting, just as I told you. Follow me – but be careful! Those who enter Inverscreech Castle should be wary. Those walls contain some deep, dark secrets.'

As they approached the archway in the crumbling wall which surrounded the castle, a taxi came down the drive, and swept past them into the courtyard, knocking Miss Ravilius flying.

'What? Who?' she sat up, reaching for her glasses and hastily jamming them onto her nose as she peered at the trio who were emerging from the car.

'It's the Americans!' said Holly. 'What are they doing here?'

'I don't know,' snapped Miss Ravilius. 'But they won't be here for long, not if I have anything to do with it!'

She was about to march forwards, but the great door began to swing slowly open, creaking and groaning as if unwilling to let anyone in. When it was partly open, the door stopped, and an old man's face peered round.

Everything about the face pointed downwards. The dark, mournful eyes, the sad mouth, even the large nose: every feature looked as if it had neither the will nor the strength to lift itself into a smile. The old man said nothing; he just stood there, waiting.

The Americans glanced at each other, and then the woman stepped forward with a huge, dazzling smile. 'Well, hi there! I'm Connie Petrucci. I believe you're expecting us.' She motioned first to the tall man. 'This is Hal Bernstein and this is Oscar Ramone. We've hired your castle.'

The old man came dramatically to life. He straightened up, his eyes flashed fire, his nostrils flared, and if he'd had any hair it would certainly have stood on end.

'It is not my castle! I am Angus Gloom, of Glen Gloom, steward of Inverscreech in the absence of the laird. That is my right to be here – what, may I ask, is yours?'

Connie glared at him. 'We're here because Maria Montez and Josh Mackenzie have paid a big fistful of dollars to rent this place for their wedding, so why don't you just cut the eccentric old retainer routine and deal with our bags!' And with that, she pushed the door wide open and led the way in. The others followed, and the four ghosts slipped after them.

'Well,' said Connie, turning up the collar of her coat and shivering. 'You sure don't believe in wasting money on heating, do you?'

They all glanced round the hall. The panelled walls were darkened by age and smoke. The carpet was thin and fraying. There were dreary oil paintings of cows with big horns, deer with even bigger horns, and misty lakes and mountains. Men wearing yards of tartan and bristling with knives glared fiercely out of their frames. A fire flickered feebly in the huge stone fireplace. Its light didn't reach far – it didn't stand much chance against the gloomy shadows that lurked at the edges of the room.

'Are you telling me,' said Oscar in disbelief, 'that Maria has *seen* this place? And that she *liked* it? And that she actually thought it would be a good place for her *wedding*?'

'She never saw inside,' said Connie, shivering and edging closer to the fire.

'She spotted it from a helicopter on the way to a location for her last film. And she said she wanted a Scottish castle. Not just any Scottish castle, but this exact same one. Said it was "atmospheric". So I looked it up on the Internet, and it said it was a romantic 700-year-old castle, newly refurbished and available for exclusive events.'

'Refurbished? What was it like before? A roofless ruin?' said Oscar. 'And why on earth didn't they build it closer to civilisation? If there is any on this backward little island, which I *seriously* doubt. Honestly, darling, both you and your boss must be totally off your heads if you think we can make a bijou backdrop out of this place. It's full of dead animals, for goodness' sake – look!' He pointed at a huge stag's head which hung above the staircase. Then he peered more closely at one of the paintings. 'And why do they have pictures of yaks?'

'They're not yaks, Oscar – they're highland cattle,' said the other man patiently.

'Oh. Well, anyway, come on, Hal, be honest – you're the great director – what do *you* think?'

The tall man sighed. 'I'm not great, Oscar, as you well know, else I wouldn't be filming a wedding video.'

'Don't knock it, dear – it could be your gateway to greatness. Last month, Josh's pop video … this month, a video of Josh and Maria's wedding … and next month, a film starring the glorious Maria Montez!'

'I wish! But meanwhile, I have to agree with you, Oscar – it doesn't look much, does it?' Hal gazed around.

'It is not for you or anyone else to criticise the ancestral home of the MacScreech clan!' squawked Angus Gloom, clearly outraged at the Americans' lack of respect. 'This castle has tales to tell that would chill you to the bone! Blood has soaked these ancient stones – and blood will out, I tell you! Blood will out!'

'Well, thanks for that,' said Connie. 'We'll watch out for it. In the meantime, my blood's turning to ice. So turn up the fire some and give us a guided tour. We've a job to get on with.'

Oscar looked horrified. 'You mean we're seriously going to go ahead and use this place? Are you out of your microscopic mind?'

'We don't have a choice,' she said shortly. 'There's no time to find anywhere else. And even if there were, Maria wants *this* place. And what Maria wants, Maria gets. You're a stylist, Oscar, so somehow you're going to have to make with the style!'

And they all fell silent as Angus Gloom led the way up the stairs.

Holly was all set to go after them, but Miss Ravilius hauled her back. 'We don't need Gloom to show us round. I know all there is to know about this place. No, we'll go to our sleeping quarters. They're special – you're going to love them. Then, this evening, you can begin work on this … this showcase for your *extraordinary* talents.' She flashed a nasty smile at Spooker, who winced and wondered, not for the first time, why she disliked him so much.

The ghosts began to move towards the stairs.

'Oh no,' said Miss Ravilius. 'Not upstairs. That's where those ghastly people will be. *We* shall go in the opposite direction.'

'Eh?' said Goof.

'Down,' she said icily. 'There is a stairway,

but students of your ability will presumably be capable of transpartition.'

'Trans *what*?' asked Goof.

'Going through the floor,' she snapped. 'Goodness, if you three are supposed to be the clever ones, I dread to think what your classmates are like! Now, follow me, and try not to get stuck!'

As they watched, her outline wobbled confusingly and slid through the floor.

Spooker blinked. 'Was it just me,' he said, 'or did something peculiar happen just then?'

'Yeah,' frowned Goof. 'She looked different, didn't she? Just for a second, before she disappeared.'

A copper-coloured head popped up through the floor. 'Is transpartition beyond you?' Miss Ravilius demanded frostily. 'It's really a very simple procedure.'

Silently, the ghosts all concentrated and thought themselves through the floor. As their teacher had said, it wasn't a difficult thing to do, but it wasn't very comfortable either. Soon enough, though, they found themselves gazing round at an extremely inhospitable dungeon. Manacles and chains were attached to the walls. More hung down from the roof. There was an occasional squeak from a passing rat. It was an interesting room, but not a cosy one.

'What is *that*?' demanded Spooker, looking at a bed-sized wooden contraption with lots of handles and some evil-looking metal spikes.

Miss Ravilius went and patted it fondly. 'It's the Inverscreech Rack,' she said. 'It doesn't just stretch prisoners, it stabs them as well. Not enough to kill them, but it certainly hurts a bit. If you're even remotely sensitive, you'll be able to sense the agony and the pain that this room's seen. Oh yes, Inverscreech is a splendid place for haunting. And you'll enjoy sleeping in the dungeon – it'll give you lots of ideas about what to put in this video of yours. Sweet dreams!' she said brightly and disappeared.

After she'd gone, there was a silence as the ghosts looked round the room. It had a distinct shortage of beds or anything else that normal bedrooms have.

'Well,' said Spooker dismally, 'who's having the rack?'

Chapter Four

They woke some hours later after an extremely unsatisfactory and uncomfortable sleep, feeling hungry and cross.

'I had *horrible* dreams,' said Goof, rubbing his eyes.

'You too?' said Spooker. 'I dreamt I was being tortured. And all the time, there was this evil old man who watched, laughing.'

Holly looked at him. 'I dreamt just the same thing. And somebody was groaning—'

'—and cursing, in a very strong Scottish accent,' finished Goof.

They all looked at each other.

'What's going on? You've been treading in my dreams,' said Goof.

'This is the funniest school trip I've ever been on,' said Holly.

'Hilarious, isn't it?' said Goof. 'Thanks for inviting us, Spooker.'

Spooker yawned. 'No problem.'

Holly was looking thoughtful. 'Did either of you notice? There was something very strange about—'

'*About what?*' The voice seemed to be right inside Holly's head. She leapt up and whirled round ... to find herself eyeball to spectacles with Miss Ravilius, who was gazing at her expectantly.

'Nothing!' she stammered. 'Absolutely nothing! Everything's fine!'

'Good, good. I'm so glad,' said Miss Ravilius briskly. 'Now, Angus Gloom is just settling down to tell the story of the castle to Those People. I think you should go and listen. It might inspire you. It's always best to base a haunting on something that's actually happened in the house. You may have other ideas, of course ... but I think you'll find out that I'm right. Anyway, come along – no time to waste.'

'Well, that was a ... a really interesting meal, Mr Gloom.' It was Hal speaking. 'Was it ... haggis, perhaps?'

'No, of course not. Have you never had a good beef stew with dumplings before?'

'Not like that,' said Connie, who looked a little green. 'I've never eaten anything quite like that before.'

'Aye well, that's as may be. Now, you were enquiring about the stain on the floorboards of your room. That stain is a bloodstain, and it cannot be removed. To understand why that should be so, you must step back almost 600 years, to a time when clan battled against clan, and blood flowed in streams through the glens… Sit yourselves down, and I will tell you the legend of Inverscreech.'

'Blood and more blood,' muttered Connie. 'What is this guy – a vampire?'

Gloom waited while they drew chairs nearer to the fire, which had been banked up and was burning quite fiercely now. In the light of the flames, his face glowed eerily, but his deep-set eyes remained in shadow.

'The neighbouring clan,' he began, 'were the MacMurdies – though MacMurderers would be a more fitting name for them! The MacMurdies were a wild and lawless bunch, and they repeatedly attacked Inverscreech without mercy. They burnt our houses, they stole our women – and then one day, worse than that by far, they stole our cattle.

'Now, you must understand, these cattle were the pride and joy of Clan MacScreech. Their beef was the sweetest, their milk was the richest, their horns were the longest, and their coats the glossiest in Scotland and beyond. So when the MacMurdies came after the cattle of Inverscreech, vengeance was swift and it was terrible, terrible beyond all imagining.' Gloom paused, looking round at them all gravely. 'The MacScreeches swept out of this castle like a raging torrent, destroying any who dared to stand against them.'

'*So* dramatic!' whispered Oscar, spellbound.

'Many were the MacMurdies who lay dead when they had passed, their blood bathing the earth. And many were the heads that were borne back to Inverscreech, to be fixed on spikes, and displayed on the walls, for all to see and tremble at!'

'Nice guys,' commented Hal.

'Yuck!' whispered Holly.

Connie frowned. 'What, so you're saying they did the fixing thing in my room? Is that where the blood came from?'

Gloom glared at her. 'No, not in the least, not at all! The story is only just begun – there is more to come, if only you will be patient!'

'Oh,' sighed Connie, settling back into her chair. 'Pardon me.'

Gloom continued. 'For 200 years, there was war between the MacScreeches and the MacMurdies. Hatred stalked the glens, as each side thirsted for vengeance.'

At that moment, the flames from the fire suddenly shrank. A sharp wind came out of nowhere, whistling round the room. The whistle turned into an agonised wail as the rush of cold air wrapped itself round first Oscar, then Connie, then Hal, before whipping up the chimney and escaping into the night.

Spooker looked round, puzzled. It had looked like a very skilful bit of haunting, but who could have done it? Miss Ravilius, Goof and Holly looked as surprised as he was.

'Absolutely the first thing we have to do,' said Connie, shivering, 'is get some central heating and double glazing put into this place. Maria doesn't set foot in it till we do.'

'For once, darling, we're in agreement.

I just can't *imagine* what it would do to Josh's vocal chords to be in this kind of atmosphere,' said Oscar.

'Maybe,' said Hal thoughtfully. 'Or maybe we can do something with this atmosphere. Something different. After all, anyone with a bunch of money can hire a castle with comfortable chairs and glitzy drapes and jacuzzis. This place has *character*. I think I'm beginning to like it!'

Gloom was fuming. 'As I was saying…'

Connie waved a hand. 'Sorry, sorry. I think hatred was stalking the glens. Oops! There it goes!'

The thing with the wind had happened again.

Gloom smiled. 'Aye!' he said with relish. 'The spirits of the dead do not rest easy! They wish to be heard, and they *will* be heard!' He darted a very nasty look at Connie, and went on.

'The feud between the two clans continued. Until finally, 200 years on, in the time of good King James the Witchfinder, matters came to a head. The Laird of Inverscreech at that time had a daughter.

39

She was a beautiful, gentle girl, with raven hair and skin of milk and roses, and that was her name, too – Rose, the Flower of Inverscreech. She was the heart of the house. Her mother had died when she was small, and she was greatly loved by her father and her brother, and indeed by all who met her.

'One day, when she was out riding, her horse was frightened by a stoat and she was thrown to the ground. A young man heard her cry and came to her aid.'

Gloom sighed, and wiped a little tear from his eye. 'And thus it began. For he was Thomas, the son of Sir Ian MacMurdie. After that first meeting, they met often, always, of course, in secret. At first, neither knew the other's true identity, and by the time they did, it was too late. For both of them, the only life they could imagine was together. But they knew that in the eyes of the clans, a union between them was unthinkable.

'And so they came to a fateful decision. They would run away, and leave these glens of sorrow behind them. Thomas was to come to Inverscreech Castle by night, by means of a secret passage that Rose had told him of. Horses would be waiting outside, and the pair would flee under cover of darkness.'

Gloom paused to take a drink, and somewhere outside an owl hooted. The sound was unspeakably lonely and sad, and the lights flickered as if in response.

Holly looked round nervously. Odd things were happening, and she didn't understand why. Most humans thought ghostly goings on were to do with the spirits of the dead, but she knew that they were just the doings of the ghost dimension. So what was happening here? Was it something to do with Gloom? He put his glass down, and continued his story.

'But the MacMurdies had taken note of young Thomas's frequent absences, and that night they followed him. And if that was bad enough, there was worse to come.

'For Agnes Gloom, who was Rose's old nurse, and as good as a mother to her, had also become suspicious. She alerted the Laird, so that unknown to Rose, a close watch was being kept on her also. And so, when the lovers met on that fateful night, they were not alone.

'A fight broke out between the MacMurdies and the MacScreeches, and the blood of the innocent was shed. A chance sword thrust pierced the heart of the Flower of Inverscreech, and at the end of the night, she lay dead, cut down in the glowing beauty of youth, in the very room in which you are sleeping.'

'Ah!' said Connie, finally satisfied. 'So that's where the blood's from! But didn't anybody ever think to clean it? In however many hundreds of years it's been since then?'

'Many have tried, and all have failed.'

Connie opened her mouth to speak, but Gloom held up his hand to stop her. 'There is a reason, and I shall come to it!' He put more wood on the fire, and everybody, ghosts included, huddled closer.

'Young Thomas died not long after. He pined away, for sorrow. His father soon followed him, stricken with sadness and remorse. For many believed it was his sword that had cut down the Flower of Inverscreech. The Laird died too, worn out with hatred and bitterness. And his son left Inverscreech, declaring that it was a cursed place, and he wanted no further part of it. And it was laid on the Glooms to be stewards of the castle henceforth, until such time as the rift should be healed. It was their doom, their punishment for the part Agnes had played in the tragedy.'

'The doom of the Glooms,' murmured Connie. 'Lovely!'

Oscar looked reprovingly at Connie. 'And how could the – what did you call it? The rift – do tell, how could it be healed?'

'That will only happen, and the bloodstain will only disappear, when the wound is healed by love – when the heirs of Clan MacScreech and Clan MacMurdie become as one. And that will never be, for the heirs have been lost. Lost in the dark and howling gales of space and time.'

A door banged somewhere in the castle, and the windows rattled.

'Great story!' said Hal admiringly. 'And good sound effects. Don't know how you do it, but they definitely work!'

'It's really quite affecting,' said Oscar, sniffing.

'It's just so romantic! I wonder what they looked like?' said Connie.

'You do not need to wonder,' replied Gloom. 'For see … here they stand, as if alive!' With a dramatic flourish, he pulled back a tapestry which hung in an alcove beside the fire, to reveal two portraits. One showed a lovely dark-eyed girl with long black hair and a fetching smile, and the other a young man, with windswept reddish-gold locks and cheekbones like crags. They were both looking sideways, so they seemed to be gazing at each other.

'Great profiles!' said Connie admiringly.

'Gorgeous hair!' said Oscar.

Hal just stared at the pictures thoughtfully. He was frowning slightly, as if something was puzzling him.

'You may have the chance to meet them yourselves,' said Gloom. 'For they walk within the walls of this castle. They, their fathers, and my ancestor Agnes. And many of the others who lost their heads and shed their blood during the feud years.'

'Goodness,' said Connie, 'it must get very crowded.'

'That's as may be,' said Gloom, glaring at her. 'Those who sleep here say that their nights are disturbed, their dreams invaded by strange sights and sounds, and their hearts seized in the cold grip of fear.'

'Then I guess you'd better make us a hot milky drink with something strong in it. Oh, and a hot water bottle wouldn't go amiss,' said Connie, yawning.

Gloom stalked into the kitchen. The others followed him, and soon, only the ghosts were left in front of the fire.

The night was theirs.

Chapter Five

'There isn't anybody else here, is there?' said Spooker suddenly.

Goof stared at him. 'Course there is, dope. There's gloomy Angus and three barking-mad Americans. Didn't you notice?'

'No, I mean other ghosts. Where else did that wind come from? And the thing with the flames, and the lights flickering?'

'Of course there aren't any other ghosts here,' said Miss Ravilius crisply. 'Remember, it's an old building. The windows don't fit well and it's a long way from anywhere else, so the electricity supply is probably uncertain. There's no need to read anything sinister into something that's perfectly natural, Spooker. You'll be telling me next you believe all that stuff Gloom was coming out with, about the dead walking and so forth! These humans – the things they believe! No, I can assure you – the only haunting taking place in this castle will be any you do for your video.

'Talking of which, isn't it about time you got on with it?' she added. 'Meanwhile, I have a few things to do back in the ghost dimension. I'll get some food while I'm there. Make sure you have some ideas ready to show me when I come back.' And she promptly disappeared.

'Well, she's a great help, isn't she?' said Goof sourly.

'Careful,' said Holly, looking round nervously, 'she might pop back again, like she did before.'

'I suppose I'd better get some paper and stuff,' said Spooker. 'I'll just nip downstairs.'

He went through the floor and collected paper and pens. Then he looked round for another way up. Transpartition was quick, but it wasn't very comfortable. He saw a door in the corner of the dungeon. Stone steps led up from it to another door, which had a large iron key in the lock. The key turned quite easily, and Spooker opened it to find himself outside the castle. It made sense, he supposed – if you had a bunch of prisoners, it would be much better to have a separate entrance; you wouldn't want to march them through the castle to the dungeon.

Spooker looked round to work out how to get back into the castle. There was no moon. The wind moaned restlessly in the trees, and he heard the squeal of an animal somewhere beyond the castle grounds, a cry of pain that was swiftly cut short. He shivered.

Then he heard a much louder sound, coming from somewhere up above. It was laughter, but it wasn't happy laughter, it was cruel and mocking. It pealed through the night air, cutting it savagely like a knife.

Spooker looked up. There was a figure up on the battlements, gazing down towards him. Light flickered around it, illuminating its face. Spooker recognised him at once. It was the old man he'd dreamt about in the dungeon. The expression on his face was mocking and evil.

Spooker turned pale. Who was he? What was going on here? He felt a need to be back with his friends. He was beginning to understand what it must feel like to be haunted.

Rather than waste time looking for a door into the castle, Spooker forced himself painfully through the thick, stone wall – and found himself in the kitchen. From there, he ran back to the drawing room.

'You took your time,' said Goof.

'Are you all right?' asked Holly, studying his face. 'You look dreadful!'

'Have you seen anything? Did you hear the laughter?' Spooker asked when he'd caught his breath. 'A *horrible* noise. It was really nasty, and really loud. And that old man we dreamt about – I saw him, up on the battlements.'

'It was probably Angus Gloom,' said Holly thoughtfully. 'I bet he's a real joker behind all that scowling.'

'Maybe, but I don't think so. Honestly, it was really weird. Come on, I think we should go and see what's going on.'

'If it was so horrible,' said Goof, 'why don't we just keep out of the way?'

The others stared at him.

'What?' he protested. 'I don't mind scary things when I'm the one who's doing them, but this castle gives me the creeps.'

'Oh, come on,' said Spooker impatiently, 'we're wasting time.'

'All right,' sighed Goof. 'I'm right behind you. A *long* way behind you,' he added, looking round nervously as he followed them up the stairs.

But almost immediately, Spooker stopped, so quickly that Holly crashed into him, banging her nose painfully.

'What is it?' said Goof, looking round fearfully. 'What have you seen?'

'Nothing,' said Spooker. 'I've just realised I don't know where we're going.'

'Oh. Shall we go back then?' said Goof hopefully.

Before Spooker or Holly could reply, loud peals of laughter – the same terrible, mocking laughter that Spooker had heard outside – thundered all around them. As the noise died away, they heard other sounds – voices crying out in fear, voices begging for mercy, voices sobbing for sorrow, voices with strong American accents…

'What the heck is going on here?'

'Oh, for heaven's sake, let's all just calm down a little, shall we?'

'Calm down? Calm down? With that terrifying sight in front of me?'

'Oscar, pull yourself together, it's just me with my night cream on.'

Connie, Hal and Oscar were on the landing at the top of the main staircase. Connie's face was smeared with a thick layer of greenish-white goo, and Oscar was cowering behind Hal.

'Now, what *was* that racket all about?' demanded Connie. 'A girl needs her beauty sleep, you know, and this has definitely got in the way of mine.'

'And if anyone needs beauty sleep, it's you!' said Oscar.

'Peace, children, peace,' said Hal. 'Come on, I have a torch. Let's go see where the action is. I think the noise came from somewhere up above – maybe even from the roof...'

'Don't leave me behind!' squawked Oscar.

'If only we could,' muttered Connie.

Off they went along the upstairs corridor. Everyone kept close to the person in front, first Hal, then Connie and Oscar, with Holly, Spooker and Goof following close behind.

Hal shone the torch round as he went.

Suddenly, he stopped, and everyone crashed into the person – or ghost – in front of them.

'Not again!' said Holly, rubbing her nose.

'What was that? I felt something!' said Oscar, looking round fearfully.

'No, no,' said Hal. 'Look, it's over there – just by those battlements!' He pointed through a window. It was difficult to see clearly, but there was a dim glow, and shadows moving in front of it. 'Come on – we're nearly there!'

'That way? Wouldn't it be better to go … this way?' Oscar turned to look wistfully back at the way they'd come. Spooker couldn't resist it. He didn't have time for anything fancy; he simply imagined himself dressed in tartan and waving a sword, and let himself be seen.

'Aaaarrrgh!' Oscar pelted after the others. 'Wait for me! I just saw something! It was horrible! It was ten-feet tall! It was glowing! It was…'

'That was mean,' said Holly.

'Yeah,' said Spooker, chuckling, 'but it was fun!'

By the time the ghosts caught up, the

Americans were heading up a narrow spiral staircase in one of the towers.

When they reached the door at the top, Hal paused. 'Ready? This must lead onto the battlements,' he whispered grimly. 'I'm going to open the door fast, so whoever it is doesn't have the chance to get away. I'll shine the torch in their face – it'll dazzle them!'

'Are you sure you've thought this through?' said poor Oscar faintly.

Hal flung open the door and there, in the powerful beam of the torch, they saw … Angus Gloom!

'Gloom! What's going on? That laughter – was it you?'

Gloom looked at Hal scornfully. 'Use your head, man. Of course it wasn't me. Look – look over there!'

The battlements were lit up in the strange orange light which Spooker had glimpsed from the grounds. Up here it was much brighter and fiercer – so much so that they all instinctively fell back, as if they were in front of a fire.

'There!' said Connie. 'What's that on the battlements?'

It was a dark shape, something that looked like a black bundle on a pole.

'Here – let me look!' It was Hal. He plunged through the light show and reached out to grasp the pole. But his hand went straight through it. He stared at his hand, and gasped, 'Did you see that?'

But none of the others were taking any notice. Instead, they were gazing in horror at the sight in front of them. It was a head, stuck on top of what must have been a sharpened stake. Blood dripped from its severed neck.

As they watched, the head began to revolve slowly to face them. It seemed like ages before they could finally see what it looked like. Oscar whimpered and hid his face behind Connie, who hid behind Hal, but couldn't resist peeking. Holly and Goof would have hidden behind Spooker, but he wasn't big enough.

The skin was blistering and peeling. The eyes, glistening in the light from the fire, were bulging and inflamed. First one and then the other popped out and slowly rolled down the cheeks, which were bubbling like a mixture in some hellish cauldron.

The mouth widened into a wild grin, and then it opened, and they heard the crazy laughter again, echoing round the turrets and battlements of the ancient castle.

'I wish I could get that on film,' said Hal. 'It's fantastic! Talk about special effects! Whoever's responsible could name his own price in Hollywood...'

No one answered, and when he turned to see why, he realised he was almost alone.

But not quite. There was a boy there, who also seemed to be watching the gory display with interest rather then fear.

'Yes,' said Spooker, quite forgetting that Hal wasn't supposed to be able to see him. 'It was good, wasn't it? The bit with the eyes, it reminded me of someone.'

'Yes, I liked that bit too ... but hey, who are you?'

Gloom, who had stepped back inside the door, wondered what to do. The shock must have unhinged the American director, because he was standing there talking to thin air. It wasn't surprising. Gloom had seen some strange sights in the castle, but he'd never seen anything like tonight's display. He cleared his throat, 'Come away in, sir,' he said. 'Perhaps a wee dram would be in order.'

Hal glanced at him, irritated. 'What?' He looked round. 'Now where did that kid go? Didn't you see him? Just a little guy – he must have gone right past you... Oh, never mind.' And he went impatiently down the stairs after the others.

Chapter Six

The Americans were all gathered back in the drawing room.

'That's it,' said Connie. 'Josh and Maria cannot get married in this hellhole. Absolutely no way.'

Hal shrugged. 'What Maria wants, Maria gets. Place just needs tidying up a little.'

'Tidying up? *Tidying up*? It's haunted, Hal, face it! And not by a nice class of ghost, either!'

'Hmm. I'm not so sure about that,' said Hal, gazing thoughtfully at Holly, Spooker and Goof. 'They might not be so bad. Anyway, the show's over for tonight. Why don't you go to bed and get some shut-eye? It'll all look better in the morning, you'll see.'

Looking round fearfully, and clutching each other for safety, Connie and Oscar went off. After producing tiny glasses of whisky, Gloom had also withdrawn.

Hal leaned forward, and stared directly at Spooker. 'Now in all those stories Gloom told us, there no mention of three ghosts who look exactly like school kids. I think you'd better tell me who you are, what's going on, and how you're doing it.'

'You can see us!' gasped Holly.

'Well, obviously, otherwise I wouldn't be talking to you. I almost saw you at the station in Edinburgh, when the other two were arguing, but then I lost sight of you and I thought my eyes must have been playing tricks on me. But I'm a director. My eyes don't play tricks on me. Ever. And then again, earlier, I almost saw you, but you always seemed to be just out of sight. But I guess you took your eye off the ball or something, because now there you are, large as life and at least half as natural. Now come on, spill. What's going on?'

So Spooker began to explain. He explained about the ghost dimension, and the Anne Boleyn Secondary School, and the inspection and the video. It took quite a while.

'So that's it,' he said finally. 'Except I don't know why you can see us. I've only ever met one other person who could,' he said, remembering Ben, the boy from his practical haunting exam.

'I guess it's a family thing,' said Hal. 'My grandmother used to talk about the ghosts she saw in her house. Mom always said she was loopy, but she never seemed loopy to me. You know, this is all a bit difficult to take in ... here I am, having a friendly chat with a bunch of kids who just happen to be ghosts.' He shook his head, as if to clear it. 'But I can't deny the evidence of my own eyes. Anyway, tell me about tonight's little exhibition – are you sure you didn't arrange that?'

Holly shook her head. 'And there shouldn't be any other ghosts here. I felt really scared. It was just like the kind of haunting Sir Rupert always wanted us to do.'

Hal looked puzzled, so then they had to tell him some more about Sir Rupert's little ways. After that it was really late, and Hal said he'd have to go to bed. They'd given him a lot to think about. He'd sleep on it, and see them tomorrow.

'Didn't Miss Rave-up say she was going to

bring us some food?' said Goof. 'I wish she'd get a move on, I'm starving.'

Spooker frowned. 'I was in the kitchen earlier. There's food there. I don't know why she needed to fetch more.'

Just then, Miss Ravilius began to appear. But her image wavered and vanished again. The ghosts looked at each other, puzzled. That kind of thing tended to happen when you were just learning how to skip dimensions; it shouldn't have been a problem for an experienced ghost.

In a couple of minutes, Miss Ravilius was back again, patting her hair nervously and adjusting her glasses. 'A spot of turbulence,' she said, not looking at them. 'You sometimes get it in this part of Scotland. It's to do with the snow.'

'Snow? But it's only September,' said Spooker.

'Don't try to be clever, Spooker,' Miss Ravilius said icily. 'It really doesn't suit you. It's much colder in the north. And haven't you ever heard of freak weather conditions?'

'Did you bring the food, Miss?' said Goof. 'Only—'

'Food? Oh, yes, of course – I must have left it on the counter.' Miss Ravilius looked round distractedly. 'One moment—' And off she went again, returning almost instantly with a carrier bag of pre-wrapped sandwiches and chocolate bars. 'There. Now, how's the whatsit – the video – getting on?'

The ghosts looked at each other.

'Well, there hasn't been much time for that,' said Holly. 'You see—'

'What? No, I don't see. I left you with a very simple instruction, and I'm at a loss to know why you haven't followed it. Well, I'm off for a rest now – it's very tiring, struggling through all this turbulence. You've got another couple of hours before daybreak. Get on with it. And remember – it should be based on something that's actually happened. But that won't be difficult. There was plenty to work on in that story of Gloom's.'

'Well, how do you like that!' said Goof, staring after her. 'She didn't even want to hear what's been going on.'

'Maybe she didn't need to,' said Spooker, slowly.

'What do you mean?'

'I've been thinking. We've seen several bits of haunting, haven't we? First there were the lights and the icy cold draught and all that. Well, she was there with us then, but she could have done simple stuff like that without any of us noticing. Then there was the big set piece, on the battlements. She wasn't with us then – but now it's all over she's turned up. Bit of a coincidence, don't you think? And there have been other things—'

'Her eyes!' said Holly excitedly. 'I saw them, remember, when she took off her glasses at the station. They were all red. And the trick with the eyes on the head on the battlements—' She fell silent, looking puzzled.

'Yes, yes,' spluttered Spooker. 'Don't you see?'

'See what?' said Goof, looking from one to the other. 'I stopped looking when his eyes popped out.' He fell silent, thinking.

'Yes − when they popped out and rolled down his cheeks. Now who does that remind you of?'

'Sir Rupert,' said Goof, bewildered. 'But I still don't get it. I thought you were saying Miss Ravilius has been behind the haunting. What's Sir Rupert got to do with it?'

'A lot!' said Spooker. 'They're one and the same ghost, don't you see? She's him, and he's her. He's been pretending to be her all this time!'

'Exactly!' said Holly excitedly. 'It all fits. Every time she fades or comes back, there's a sort of wobbly moment where she doesn't look like herself − and that's because it must be really difficult to do transpartition and hold on to being Miss Ravilius at the same time!'

'And she's doing the haunting,' Spooker reminded her. 'No wonder she's, or rather he's, so tired.'

'Hold on, hold on,' said Goof, frowning in concentration. 'I still don't understand. If it – she – is him, then *why*? Why is he doing it? Why is he here and not in Hollywood?'

They sat in silence, thinking. At last, Spooker stirred. 'Perhaps he wants to get his own back on us because of losing his job. Perhaps he's just jealous and wants to stop us from making the video.'

'Or maybe he's just mad,' suggested Holly. 'I mean, he was always on the edge of it. Perhaps you just tipped him over.'

They all sat and thought about being stranded in a lonely Scottish castle, hundreds of miles from home, with a deranged Sir Rupert.

'I wonder what he'll do next?' said Holly, looking worried.

Spooker sighed. 'I don't know. I can't think. I'm shattered. Let's get some sleep. But not in that dungeon – he must have put us there just so he could give us bad dreams. I want a nice comfortable bed, in a proper bedroom…'

In another part of the castle, Sir Rupert flung himself onto his bed. He had never for a moment thought it would be as hard as this. There were times when he hardly knew who he was or what he was doing. The Americans didn't help, particularly Hal. He had no respect, none at all, and it was very difficult to concentrate with him watching in that cool, calm, superior way he had.

Yes, Sir Rupert was absolutely worn out. But it would be worth it. It would all be worth it. If he could have the satisfaction of proving to that smug little pipsqueak – and Chalky White, and all the other incompetent softies who taught at the Anne Boleyn Secondary School – that in the end, all this new-fangled nonsense was just that: complete and utter rubbish. Because it was as he'd always said, to all those generations of pupils he'd taught successfully for so many years: terror was what counted. Heart-stopping, blood-freezing, marrow-churning terror. And that was exactly what he was going to supply tomorrow. By the bucketload.

He closed his eyes, and slipped into an exhausted sleep.

Chapter Seven

It was evening. Spooker woke and stretched. He'd slept much better than the previous night, and there had been no nightmares. In fact, he had the feeling there might have been a rather nice dream, but all he could remember about it was the smell. It was a smell of summer, of flowers perhaps, and it still seemed to be lingering in the room.

He sat up and looked round. All he'd noticed the night before was the big four-poster bed, but now he was curious about his surroundings. There was a carved wooden chest at the foot of the bed, and a chair and a table. But the main thing that drew his attention was a portrait above the fireplace. It was of an elderly man, draped in yards of tartan and striking a heroic pose.

With a start, Spooker realised that it was the old man he'd dreamt about and then seen on the battlements. But in this portrait, he looked very different. This man didn't look evil or cruel. He just looked incredibly sad, as if he'd lost everything and everyone he'd ever cared about.

On impulse, Spooker got off the bed and went over to the picture and touched the figure. 'I'm sorry,' he said. 'I don't know why you're so sad, but I'm sorry for it.'

Then he noticed there was a small silver label fixed to the picture frame, and looking more closely, he saw what it said: *The Last Laird of Inverscreech.* He must be Rose's father.

The window was open, and a light breeze stirred the curtains. The smell of flowers grew stronger, and Spooker looked round. The door opened, and Holly came in. 'Oh,' he said, 'was that you?'

'What?' she said.

'The smell – a sweet smell – of flowers or something,' he added hastily.

Holly shook her head. 'No, but I noticed it too. It's much stronger here than in my room. Do you think it's anything to do with Sir Rupert?'

'Doesn't seem like his kind of thing, does it? Much too nice. It must just be the garden.'

After they'd woken Goof and eaten some sandwiches, the ghosts went to look for Hal. Spooker wanted to tell him what they'd discovered about Sir Rupert and Miss Ravilius. They came across Connie and Oscar first, sitting in the dining room. The table was covered with sketches, pieces of material and photographs, a laptop and two mobile phones. Connie and Oscar seemed so miserable that they couldn't even be bothered to squabble.

'You're sure Maria won't change her mind?' said Oscar. 'I've been looking on the Internet – there are loads of totally gorgeous castles. The Highlands are positively *littered* with them. There's one here with its own golf course and gym, and divine themed bedrooms and a well brought up, *regular* kind of a ghost.'

'Who's that?' asked Connie.

'Mary Queen of Scots. Not some disgusting anonymous head on a stick with a nasty eye disease and a warped sense of humour.'

Connie sighed. 'It's no good. Maria won't budge. She says she has a feeling about this place. A *feeling*!' She rolled her eyes in despair. 'I've spent the whole day trying to get hold of decorators and florists and … oh, all the zillions of people we're going to need to transform this place. Everybody's busy. *Nobody* wants to come all the way out here – well, not at this short notice. I'm beginning to believe in Gloom's curse.'

The ghosts looked at each other. Things were clearly not going well. They went to see how Hal was getting on.

Hal was standing at the foot of the great staircase. He had a camera in his hand and he was turning round slowly, looking through the viewfinder, trying out different angles.

'Er, hello,' said Spooker.

Hal grinned at them. 'Oh, it's the spooks. Hi, guys.' Then he paused and said, as if to himself, 'I can't believe I said that. I can't believe I'm talking to a bunch of ghosts just as if they were ordinary kids.'

'But we *are* ordinary kids,' said Goof cheerfully. 'It's just we're in a slightly different dimension. Or something. I don't really understand the physics,' he added.

'Are you going to make a film?' asked Holly.

'Not exactly. I'm just thinking about some shots I might use for the wedding video. This could be my big break – Maria might be interested in doing a film I've talked to her about, but she asked if I'd do her wedding video first. So of course I said yes. She's the kind of star – the big name I need – to get my film off the ground.'

'The other two don't seem very happy about the castle,' said Spooker.

'No, I know. But Maria's set on it. And, you know—' he broke off and looked at the high ceilings and the intricately carved staircase.

'What?' said Holly.

'I think it could be just fine. It's full of atmosphere. Only at the moment, it's the *wrong* kind of atmosphere. What with the laughing head and all, it's not the kind of entertainment we want at a wedding reception...'

'We might be able to help you,' said Spooker, 'and perhaps you could help us, too. I think I might have a plan,' he added modestly.

Hal looked at them. 'You'd better tell me,' he said. 'Four heads are better than three.' And he sat down on the stairs to listen.

Holly told him their suspicions about Sir Rupert, and then Spooker took a deep breath and began to explain his plan.

'I think this castle has a bad atmosphere because of Sir Rupert,' he said. 'Take the old man – Sir Rupert makes him horrible and cruel, but if you look at that portrait in my room, he's not really like that at all. He's just sad – really, really sad. If we put on a different kind of haunting, then maybe we can sort of drown out what Sir Rupert's doing.'

Holly looked excited. 'It could work!'

Goof was less sure. 'You mean a competition? Between us and Sir Rupert? You think we could win?'

'Well, we might. You never know...' Spooker tried to look confident.

'It's worth a try,' said Hal. 'After all, from what you've told me, you've beaten him before. Let's go for it! Now, how can I help?'

'Well, if you didn't mind, I thought you could video what we do and then give us a hand editing it,' said Spooker. 'We came here to make a video for Ofghost, and so far we haven't got anywhere with it. So it would be great if you could help us to get it done.'

'No problem! So all we have to do now is plan the routine, is that right? OK, let's go...'

Chapter Eight

A little later, Spooker, Goof and Holly were sitting in the library, gathered round a notebook, when Miss Ravilius appeared through the wall looking cross and dishevelled. Her hair was falling down around her face, and her blouse was no longer neatly tucked in. The strain was definitely showing.

'I've been looking all over for you,' she snapped. 'What are you doing in here?'

'We've been doing a storyboard,' said Holly calmly. 'For the video. We came in here to keep out of the way of the Americans. And, well, it is a library, isn't it? It seemed a good place to work.'

'I see – a storyboard, you say?'

'Yes, look. We'll start off with an introduction from Spooker. Then it'll cut to Holly, saying that we're going to demonstrate happy haunting by—'

'You're going to demonstrate *what*?'

'*Happy haunting*,' said Goof proudly. 'That's what we're going to call the video. It's a great title, isn't it? I thought of it. Well, I think it was me—'

Miss Ravilius glared at him.

'Well, as I was saying,' Goof went on, 'Holly will explain that we're going to show what we mean by producing a haunting that will bring peace and happiness to even a gloomy place like this.'

'Peace? Happiness?' Miss Ravilius looked like thunder. 'Do you *still* think that's what haunting's all about? You'll have to excuse me, I feel a little sick. I think I need a lie down…'

'See you later,' murmured Spooker, as she shot off through the wall.

'Right,' said Holly briskly. 'We'd better get ready. There's a lot to do.'

But suddenly, a humming sound which they'd hardly noticed became louder, and then much louder, until it seemed to be filling the whole sky and encircling the castle. They ran over to the window, just in time to see a helicopter landing in the field just beyond the grounds. Two figures climbed out, ran out of range of the whirling blades, and waved as the helicopter took off again, banking steeply and flying off towards the sun. Then the figures linked arms and came towards the castle.

Intrigued, the three ghosts hurried to see what was happening. The two people arrived at the front entrance, where Connie and

Oscar were waiting to meet them, with Angus Gloom hovering in the background.

'Connie!' The girl broke away and ran towards them She had long, red–gold hair, which flew out behind her catching the rays of the setting sun, so that it looked almost as if it was on fire. 'Isn't it great? You sounded in such a state we thought we'd better come and see the place for ourselves. Josh, don't you just love it?'

The man, tall and dark-haired, was standing staring at the castle. 'It's the oddest thing,' he said slowly. 'I feel as if I've been here before. And yet I know I haven't.'

There was a loud thud. Angus Gloom had hit the floor in a dead faint.

'Goodness,' said Maria, gazing at Angus with interest. 'Do you think we should fan him? Or throw water over him or something? Who is he, anyway?'

Gloom stirred and sat up. He looked shaky, and he had a very odd expression on his face, which Spooker suddenly realised was a smile. He gawped at Maria, and then beyond her at Josh, who had also come inside and was gazing round the great entrance hall, looking slightly puzzled. Then without saying a word, and ignoring the hands held out to help him up, Gloom scrambled to his feet and scuttled off.

'He's the steward. Kind of a caretaker,' said Connie. 'He's an eccentric kind of a guy. Anyway, never mind him, come on through, and we'll catch up. This is the weirdest place – really, you have no idea…'

After they'd gone, the ghosts looked at each other.

'Does this change things?' said Holly.

'No,' said Spooker cheerfully. 'It just means we'll have a bigger audience. Come on. We need to sort out exactly what each of us is going to do.'

Chapter Nine

Later that night, everything was in place. The castle was silent, and all the young ghosts had to do was wait. They knew that something was going to happen and when it did, they would be ready. In the meantime, they sat playing cards in the library.

'Listen!' said Spooker. 'Can you hear something?'

'Look!' whispered Holly, fascinated. 'That section of bookshelves – it's moving!'

'Haunted bookshelves – that's new!' murmured Goof.

'No, you twit, it must be the way in from the secret passage – the one that Rose and Thomas used. It looks like Sir Rupert's going to show the last bit of the story, the bloody bit. Remember to look scared!'

A silvery funnel of icy mist swirled in through the gap revealed by the slowly opening section of shelves. The mist wrapped itself round the three ghosts like a freezing blast, and then solidified into the appearance of four men, fierce and savage-looking, wearing tartan and armed with swords and cudgels. They grew larger, and loomed over Spooker, Goof and Holly, grinning horribly. One drew a finger across his throat and mouthed silently: 'Later!' Then they vanished through the door.

It wasn't that hard to look frightened.

'You've got to admit, he's good,' said Goof. 'That was a phantas-whatsit, wasn't it?'

'Phantasmagoria,' said Spooker helpfully. 'When a single ghost creates the appearance of several entities. Yes, he's good. But so are we. Come on.'

Then they shot up through the ceiling and went their separate ways.

Connie woke with a start. Something was definitely wrong. 'Oh no,' she muttered. 'Not that damn joker on a stick again!' She listened. But there were no peals of evil laughter, no orange glow lighting up the sky and, with a sigh, she snuggled back down under the covers.

But only for a moment. For then she heard a sound that, for her at least, was even worse than the mirthless screeches of the night before. Ever since she was a child, Connie had hated the sound of metal scraping on a hard surface. She remembered being on holiday once, walking behind her brother, who had a metal spade which he trailed along the pavement, making a dreadful scraping noise which set her teeth on edge. And he knew it too; he kept looking over his shoulder and beaming at her in an irritating way. This sound was like that, only ten times worse. Metal was clashing on metal, right outside her door. It was a whining, piercing kind of a sound, and it was loud – louder than she could bear.

Too furious to be frightened, Connie leapt out of bed and flung open the door, determined to do whatever was needed to stop the terrible noise that was sending shockwaves through her ears. But not a squeak came out of her, let alone a scream. For outside her room, the passageway was full of savage-looking, see-through clansmen wielding huge swords, which might have been spectral but still appeared horribly sharp. A severed hand flew towards her, trailing drops of blood. It seemed to be heading straight towards her face, and the gnarled fingers and uncut, yellowing nails looked set to claw her eyes out.

'Oh, for crying out loud,' she said in disgust as she ducked, then turned to see the hand disintegrate into silvery particles.

Then there was a sharp cry. It was a girl's voice, and it was a cry of pain.

'Maria?' whispered Connie. 'Is that you?'

The noise quietened, and the fighting figures faded, leaving only an old man, bending over a figure which lay on the floor. He rose, and slowly turned. Connie knew she didn't want to see him, but she couldn't look away. His face was livid, filled to the brim with fury and hatred.

The old man raised his hand, and spoke in a terrible voice:

'From this time forth, my curse, the curse of the Laird of Inverscreech, shall rest on Clan MacMurdie and all their descendants from now until the end of time! Let no—'

But suddenly another figure appeared. This, too, was an elderly man. He looked almost exactly like the other one. But the expression on his face was very different. This man didn't look angry, but incredibly sad. He stood, leaning on a stick, and gazed quietly at the other, who stared back in evident astonishment.

The second figure spoke. 'No,' he said. 'If ever there was a curse, it is no longer. The time has come for the sorrow to end. Hope and happiness have returned to Inverscreech.' He turned, and looked towards Angus

Gloom, who, along with all the other inhabitants of the castle had come out of their rooms and were watching in spellbound silence. 'The stewardship of the Glooms is over. Accept my thanks.'

There was a sigh, and another figure appeared, this time an old woman who had a distinct look of Gloom himself.

'Agnes?' whispered Gloom.

She smiled and clasped her hands. 'My boy!' she declared, with a look of pride.

'Wow!' murmured Oscar, who had crept nervously closer to Connie while the cursing was going on. 'How many more of these guys are there going to be?'

'Look at the shouty one!' said Connie. 'Does he look kind of weird to you? I mean – even weirder than he did before?'

The outline of the first old man seemed to wobble and change. He became a smaller, slightly younger-looking figure with a moustache and a rather wobbly head, and the tartan in which he was wrapped shifted and re-formed into a white ruff above a red doublet and purple breeches. There was a look of outrage on his face. He glanced round at Hal, who was filming the proceedings with a small camcorder.

'What on earth do you think you're doing?' snarled the ghost who'd wobbled.

Hal smiled slightly. 'Just a spot of filming,' he said, 'for some young friends of mine. I believe you know them, too. They're a little busy at the moment, said to say they were sorry they couldn't be here to meet you.'

The ghost howled in rage, and promptly disappeared.

Hal grinned at Agnes and the Laird. 'Well,' he said. 'I guess that's a wrap.'

But they were gazing past him, at two figures who were standing at the top of the stairs — a dark-eyed girl with long black hair, and a young man with extremely good cheekbones and tangled red-gold curls. The young man gazed at the girl and smiled, and drew her arm into his. Then the pair of them walked down the passageway to where Maria and Josh were standing. They gazed at them with great tenderness, and reached out and touched their hands. 'Like rose petals,' Maria said afterwards. 'It was just like rose petals settling on my hand.'

Josh moved forward. 'Wait,' he said, 'please wait!'

But the figures were already fading, leaving behind them a delicate scent of roses and other summer flowers, which brought smiles to the face of everyone watching.

'I knew it!' trilled Angus Gloom. 'As soon as I saw you both, I knew it!'

'Knew what?' asked Connie, feeling that someone had to.

'Can you not see it? They are the heirs! He is like the twin of the Rose of Inverscreech, and as for herself.' He pointed to Maria. 'She is exactly like the portrait of young Thomas MacMurdie. How this can be I do not know, but the truth is there for all to see – the heirs have returned, to fulfil the promise of the legend!'

Chapter Ten

Things were bubbling too much for everyone to go to bed straightaway. Josh and Maria were mystified and excited by all that had happened, and Angus Gloom had to relate the legend of Inverscreech at least twice before they could begin to grasp it. Then Josh had rung his parents in Chicago to find out if they could throw any light on the mystery. That had been simple: Josh's father had been born a MacScreech, but for obvious reasons had changed his name once he realised that he wanted a career in music. His parents were both dead, and his only relatives of that generation were three aunts who had changed their names through marriage. So Josh had never come across any relative named MacScreech.

It would take longer to unravel the truth about Maria. She had been adopted as a baby, and knew very little about her birth parents.

But there seemed little doubt that the trail would eventually lead to a MacMurdie – the family resemblance could not have been more striking.

Eventually, they all went to bed except for Hal, who came down to the library to talk to Spooker, Goof and Holly. There was a wide grin on his face. 'It was brilliant!' he said. 'Everybody's happy – Maria and Josh were anyway, but now they're over the moon. Oscar and Connie are drooling about all the publicity they'll get from the story – the papers will love it – and as for Gloom, I think he'll have to change his name. He just can't stop smiling. It's like you said – the whole atmosphere's changed. Everybody's decided it won't take much to get the castle looking good for the wedding. It suddenly all looks a whole lot easier.

'But … what happened? It wasn't quite how you planned, was it?'

'Not a bit,' confessed Spooker. 'I was going to be the Laird. But when I went back to look at the portrait, to get some inspiration, the old man was there, stepping out of his picture! I couldn't believe it. I knew it wasn't

Sir Rupert – it was the old man I'd seen before, but he looked really different, not evil at all. I didn't know what was going on – I still don't. But I followed him, and saw what you all saw.'

'Same here,' said Holly. 'Me and Goof were going to be Rose and Thomas, but they were already out of their portraits by the time we reached them. And as for Agnes, I've no idea where she came from.'

Hal nodded. 'Yes, she was a surprise. So … have I got this right? None of you were actually performing at all?'

'No,' said Spooker.

'So who—?'

They were all silent, thinking.

Suddenly, Hal sat up. 'Hey, the video! Let's see what's on there!' He picked up the camcorder, rewound the tape, and set it to play. It showed everything up to the point just before the second old man appeared. And after that, nothing. There wasn't a trace of Agnes, the second old man, or Rose and Thomas.

'Spooky, isn't it,' said Holly thoughtfully. 'You don't think … I mean, you know, all that stuff human beings believe, about ghosts being the spirits of the dead – it couldn't be true, could it?'

'Nah,' said Goof firmly. 'Course not.'

'Definitely not,' agreed Spooker. 'No chance.'

All three of them sat and stared at their feet for a bit, thinking.

'Well,' said Hal, 'whatever happened, it did the trick. But what are we going to do about your video? Hey, just a minute! What's going on *now*?' He was staring at a spot just behind the three ghosts.

Spooker, Goof and Holly whirled round, to see the air shivering and becoming solid as a figure appeared. It was Sir Rupert. He looked pale and exhausted, but there was an unmistakeable air of triumph about him.

'Ha! So I won after all! No video, no nonsense about "happy haunting", no more brownie points from the In-spectres!' he declared, with a manic gleam in his bloodshot eyes.

Hal visibly pulled himself together. Spooker, Holly and Goof were one thing. This apparition was quite another.

Hal leaned forward. 'Wrong,' he said. 'What happened back there was too strong for you, and you know it. The castle won. It's peaceful now. You didn't win. But you *are* good.' He looked at Sir Rupert, considering. 'Spooks here tells me you'd thought of going to Hollywood. Why did you change your mind?'

Sir Rupert sat down. It seemed as if all the fight had gone out of him. He'd done his very best, and it hadn't been enough. He sighed.

'I'm old. Older than you can imagine. I couldn't face the upheaval. My life was that school … till *he* took it away from me.' He shot a cruel glance at Spooker. 'So I decided I'd make a comeback. I'd have my revenge, and then everyone would see that my way was right, and they'd beg me to go back.'

'But it hasn't worked out like that, has it?' said Hal kindly. 'So I have a suggestion to make. Forget the school. Come to Hollywood with us. Someone with your ability – you'll be turning parts down, believe me. Though you might want to consider a slight change of image when you're not actually on camera,' he added hastily, as Sir Rupert's rather startling eyes lit up like red lanterns.

'Do you really mean it?' he said nervously. It had been at least 150 years since anyone had been kind to him.

'Yes,' said Hal firmly, 'but there is a condition. I'm going to help these kids with their video, and I don't want any interference from you. Is it a deal?'

And so it was all agreed. The following week, Spooker, Goof and Holly were back at school. Their 'Happy Haunting' video was shown at a special presentation evening, and everyone was delighted with it. There were more pictures in the paper, and the three of them bought a copy one morning before school.

'We look good, don't we?' said Goof, admiring his picture. 'Don't you think so, Holly? Holly…?'

But Holly was looking at the shelf that had human magazines on it — ghosts found them useful for reference. 'Look at this one!' she said. 'It's got loads of pictures of Josh and Maria's wedding in it!'

The wedding itself had taken place outside in the castle grounds, lit by soft gold evening sunlight, with a backdrop of heather-covered hills. Josh was wearing tartan, and Maria wore a dress just like the one in Rose's portrait. She carried roses, and there were more in her hair.

Holly peered more closely at one of the pictures. 'Look!' she said. 'There, near the back. That's Gloom, isn't it? But beside him — isn't it…?'

It *was* Sir Rupert. The image was fuzzy, and it was odd to see him wearing a suit, but it was definitely him.

'Wow,' said Goof. 'Both he and Gloom are smiling. I don't know which of them looks more weird.'

'I wish we could have been there,' said Holly wistfully.

'Mmm. Still, Hal said he'd send us tickets for the premiere of the film he's making with Maria, didn't he? Shame it won't be for a while though,' said Spooker.

They bought some sweets, and strolled back to school. It was to be their first lesson with the new practical haunting teacher that afternoon.

'Wonder what he'll be like,' said Holly.

Spooker grinned. 'I don't know, but whoever it is, they'll have a hard act to follow!'

About the author

I come from Derbyshire, which is a lovely county with lots of hills in the northern part – the Peak District. I, however, lived in the less lovely bit between Derby and Nottingham. I went to university in Durham, and then worked in London and Leicester before moving to Somerset. I still live there, and divide my time between teaching (sort of) and writing books for children.

The first of these, *Spook School*, was published in 2003, and featured a dreadful character called Sir Rupert Grimsdyke, who I later realised had a great deal in common with someone who used to teach me at Ilkeston Grammar School.

Changing Brooms, which was about a house makeover TV programme for witches, came along the following year, and now with *Spooks Away* I've come back to the parallel world of the ghosts which appeared in *Spook School*.

When I was little, we used to watch old films on TV on Sunday afternoons. My parents would fall asleep, and I would sit there wishing there was something more exciting to do.

But one Sunday, there was an even older film than usual. It was about a haunted Scottish castle, which was sold to an American and transported across the Atlantic stone by stone, much to the annoyance of the resident ghost. It was meant to be a funny film, but actually I found the ghost very scary. It seemed very real, and the castle was very spooky indeed.

I think that memory, lurking in my brain like the monster at the bottom of Loch Ness, was what made me send Spooker and his friends to Scotland for their second outing. I thought they'd find plenty of adventures there, and I turned out to be right...